Agnon's Alef Bet

*I*n honor of Hebrew teachers and their students,
this volume was made possible by a grant
from the family of
Chana and Yaakov Yosef Kekst z"l
whose lives were lovingly devoted to the study and teaching of Hebrew.

Agnon's Alef Bet

POEMS BY
S.Y. AGNON

Translated by Robert Friend

Illustrated by
ARIEH ZELDICH

The Jewish
Publication
Society
PHILADELPHIA
JERUSALEM

1998 · 5758

Manufactured in Hong Kong

Library of Congress Cataloging-in-Publication Data

Agnon, Shmuel Yosef, 1888–1970.
   (Sefer ha-otiyot. Hebrew)
   Agnon's Aleph Bet: poems/by S. Y. Agnon; translated by Robert Friend; illustrated by Arieh Zeldich.
        p. cm.
   English and Hebrew.
   Summary: Presents poetry based on the Hebrew alphabet with one poem for each letter.
   ISBN 0-8276-0599-4
   (1. Hebrew language—Alphabet. 2. Alphabet. 3. Hebrew language materials—Bilingual.) I. Friend, Robert. II. Zeldich, Arieh, 1949– ill. III. Title.
PJ5053.A41413   1998
892.4' 15—dc21
                     97-38777
                     CIP
                     AC HE

---

98 99 00 01 02 10 9 8 7 6 5 4 3 2 1

Designed by NACHMAN ELSNER

*T*ranslating from one language to another is always a challenge, especially when the original text is written by a consummate literary craftsman like Nobel Prize laureate S. Y. Agnon.

With the kind assistance of Robert Friend, a world-renowned poet and translator, JPS is proud to offer a faithful English translation of Agnon's poems that is sensitive to the nuances and word-play of the original text. To assist readers with the text, Friend has provided helpful notes on the pages immediately following the English poems. These notes explain the relationship of the original Hebrew to the letters of the alef bet that give each poem its title and theme.

For readers interested in the original Hebrew text, JPS has reprinted Agnon's poems as they originally appeared in Schocken's Hebrew edition, beginning at the back of the book. We wish to thank Schocken Israel for their kind permission to reprint this material.

*I*n the original Hebrew, the letter of the alphabet gives each particular poem its title and central theme. This relationship between letter and poem (with several exceptions explained in the notes following the English poems) is mostly centered on a word that is often identical or similar in sound to that letter, although not necessarily similar in meaning. These similarities cannot be reproduced in English, hence these notes to assist the reader. I have in every poem emphasized by means of CAPITAL LETTERS the key word when it makes its first appearance.

—R.F.

TRANSLATOR'S DEDICATION
AND ACKNOWLEDGEMENTS

*T*hese translations are dedicated to the memory of my Aunt Yetta, who opened the world of the Bible to me.

I want to thank Shimon Sandbank, Anat Levin, and Ruth Nevo for helping me make sense of Agnon's sometimes complex Hebrew. My thanks go out as well to Carol Efrati for her fruitful suggestions and for her proofreading.

Shimon Sandbank proved especially helpful by going over the manuscript with great care, not only catching errors but also making suggestions that improved my translations considerably.

—R.F.

Agnon's Alef Bet

Alef ∾ א

Sometimes by candlelight
Little Uriel likes to sit
With a book of the ALPHABET
And thinks as he looks through it:

Letters! So many, so many.
He counts them. Twenty-two!
But an angel from heaven whispers:
This is what you must do.

Learn a letter today,
Tomorrow another one,
And soon you will get to be
As wise as Solomon.

Bet ⟋ ב

*F*our hundred and eighty years it took
Since the Jews left Egypt land
For Solomon to see at last
His holy TEMPLE stand.

Seven long years it took
To build the Temple (Amen),
And to hew the stones and carry them,
Eighty thousand men.

Seventy-thousand men it took
To set the bricks with plaster,
While others standing over them
Cried, "Faster, faster, faster!

For we are building a HOUSE for God
Upon the highest hill."
So on they worked, and working sang—
A singing we hear still.

Gimmel ~ ג

*N*oah built himself an Ark,
Noah, a man upright,
And caulked its cedarwood with pitch
To make it watertight.

And two of every living thing,
The female and the male,
Both fowl and beast came to the Ark
Before it could set sail.

And two of every living thing,
As fast as they could go
Came to the Ark to be on time
But the CAMEL, he went slow.

Camel, camel, hurry up.
Put Noah's mind at rest.
He's peering through the porthole now
Looking quite distressed.

And the camel, strong as he was and tall,
Embarrassed scratched his head,
But too excited to hold his tongue
Stuttered as he said:

"Good Noah, there still remains on land
The crippled who can't be rushed;
A grasshopper and a locust, too,
And a bird whose wing is crushed.

So Noah, please wait patiently
Though the sky is getting dark.
I'm lifting them all upon my hump
And bringing them to the Ark."

Dalet ⟋ ד

Joseph ruled in Egypt,
The people were unfed.
It was a time of famine
And they came to ask for bread.

And they came to Joseph,
And lying at his feet
Offered gold and silver
In exchange for wheat.

Among them came his brothers
To plead on bended knee,
But though you keep on asking,
Them you will not see.

They're all inside his palace,
So, as I said before,
You will not get to see them,
Though you get to see the DOOR.

Heh 〰ה

When ABEL was a shepherd
In the days of long ago,
He heard a lost lamb bleating
As it wandered to and fro.

As if she were a child of his,
True shepherd of his sheep,
He gave her water, gave her food,
Then tired, lay down to sleep.

Vav ׳

*T*he Israelites, told to bring
Each an offering
For the Sacred Tent,
Brought boards of acacia wood,
For the Ark of the Covenant,
Brought boards to erect the posts
All lined with copper and gold
And fitted with ring after ring—
HOOKS for the fastening
Of curtains of linen and lace,
Linens blue, purple and red,
Run through with golden thread—
To set off the Holy Place.

Bring, said the Lord as well,
Ram skin and goat hair
And the skin of the gazelle
To line the sides of the tent,
The Tent, Tent, Tent
Of the Ark of the Covenant.

Bezalel sat in thought
And wrought, wrought, wrought
What the Lord had told,
Working his copper and bronze,
Hammering out the gold.

Zayin ⌇ ז

The dove flew north
And the dove flew south.
Is that an OLIVE leaf
In its mouth?

The leaf was a letter
From an olive tree
Sent to Noah
Lost on the sea.

He took the letter
In his hand
From the Mount of Olives
In the Holy Land.

"Come," said the letter,
"It is time to rest.
Come build your house
In the land of the blessed."

Het ∩

*T*HE night had not yet passed,
The day had not yet come
When Joseph woke at last,
Woke from his fearful DREAM,
Still trembling and struck dumb,
Woke to darkest night
Without a single gleam.
To a silence so profound,
He could hear no voice or sound.
No, nothing more
Than the waves as they whispered
To the sands upon the shore.
But suddenly from a cloud,
Moonlight as bright as day
Came breaking through.
And Joseph the dreamer saw,
Shining like seraphim,
Eleven stars in heaven
Bowing low to him,
And the moon and the sun bowed, too.

Waking he looked left,
Waking he looked right,
Wherever Joseph looked,
He saw nothing but night.
He listened but heard no voice,
He listened but heard no sound.
His brothers were sunk
In a sleep so profound,
It seemed they would never
Wake from their sleep.
Only he was awake,

Still trembling from his dream
When breaking through a cloud
As from a shroud,
He saw the moonlight gleam,
And by its sudden light,
As if they were seraphim
The moon, the sun, eleven stars
All bowing low to him.

He looked at his brothers,
He looked at a star,
The face of each brother
Was that of a star.
The face of a star
Was that of each brother.
And when the moon broke
As from a shroud
Out of a cloud,
The face of his mother
Shone like the sun.
His mother was dead.
How *could* she be here!
Can the sun shine bright
In the dead of night!
His brothers would hate him.
What was this dream?
What did it mean
That older than he,
They bowed low before him,
To worship and adore him?

Tet ט

And Joseph was hurled
Into a pit.
Seven-headed serpents
Were lying in it.

And the serpents curled
Like a *Zayin* or *Het*
And one at his ear
Curled like a TET.

And the snake curled there
Whispered and hissed,
And without lying
It whispered this:

Don't be afraid.
God for your sake
Makes harmless the scorpion,
Makes harmless the snake.

Yod ✍ י

And in the Last of Days,
The innocent wolf and lamb
Will come to a Rabbi's school
To learn what they can—
Beasts of the field will come
And beasts that no longer prey
To study the Bible
And the Prayer Book all day.
Lion and leopard,
Vulture and vole,
From mountain and meadow,
From cave and from hole.
There in the Rabbi's class
Where love is the weather,
They will chant in one tongue
Their lessons together.
Even a child
Will sit in that school,
His hand stretched out
To stroke serpent or mule,
The beasts that slither,
Or the beasts that run.
We have finished with YOD now.
This story's done.

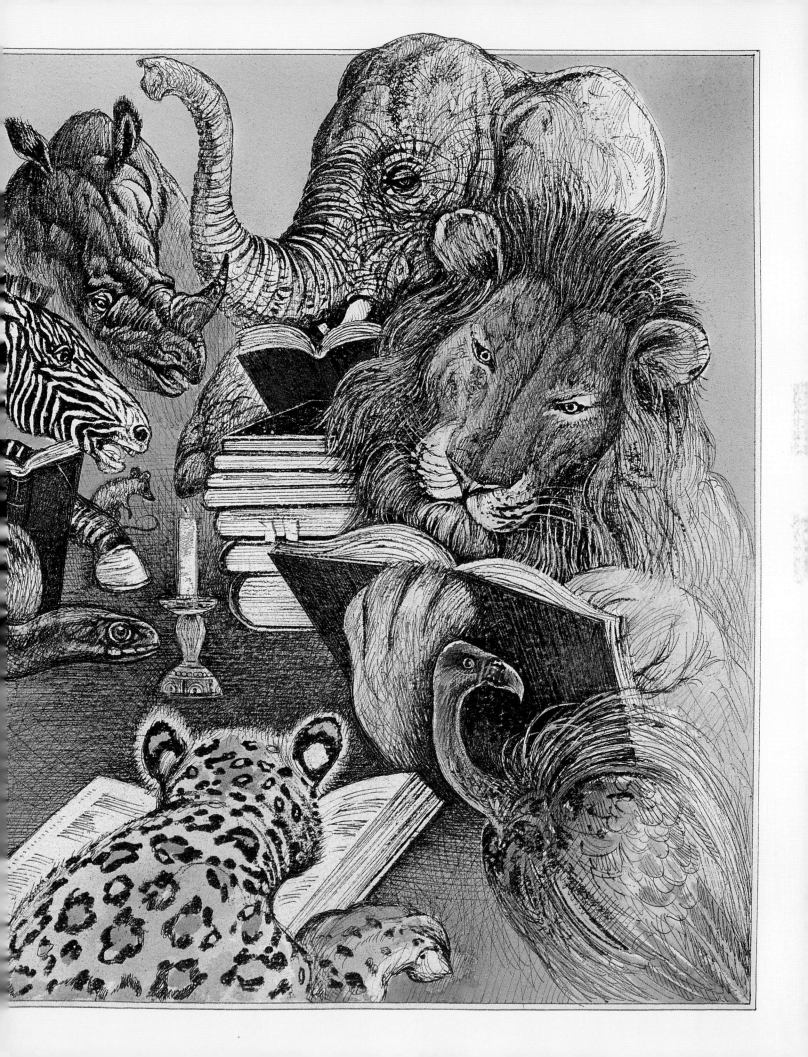

Kaf ⟋ כ

A pan of the scales—
One up, one down
The Chaldeans fight
In Jerusalem town.

See the pan up,
See the pan down,
Jeremiah dragged off
To Babylon.

See the pan down,
See the pan rise.
God gave his word
Not once, but twice.

One pan up,
One pan down,
Buy a field
Near Jerusalem town.

One pan up,
One pan down,
You will have fields
In Jerusalem town.

God's word in the pan,
God's mercy to man,
Keeping his eye on
His people and Zion.

Lamed ☙ ל

"A Philistine has stolen
The flax from my field,
And a fox has eaten
And thinned out my yield."

And Samson called out, and from left and from right
Three hundred foxes came out of the night,
Tails waving in fear, but their eyes shining bright.

For Samson in anger had thought of a ruse,
And had tied—tail to tail—the foxes by twos,
And fastened between their tethered backs
TORCHES made of sulphur and flax.
Then setting the torches all aflame,
He drove the foxes in God's name
Into the fields of the Philistines,
To burn their wheat and burn their vines.

How beautiful, o foxes,
Pace after pace,
The flags and the flames
Of your tails as you race!

O foxes, rejoice
As you run left and right
Towards hay stack and field
To light up the night.

There where the wheat
Burns to the ground,
Dance and let
Your voices resound.
The shadows flee
As the torches flame,
Light for the Jews
In Samson's name!

Mem ⟨⟩ מ

Down to the Nile
To fetch water
Went the wise MIRIAM
To bring back water,
Water water
To bathe her brother
Little MOSES.

She went far
To fill her jar
With water water.
The wise Miriam
Brought back water
To bathe her brother
Little Moses.

Nun

Noah, son of Noah,
And the son of Noah's son
Can find no rest
Under the sun.
Here come the locusts—
Cloud after cloud,
Beyond all belief—
Munchers and crunchers,
Rippers and strippers
Of every green leaf.

In the blink of an eye
A mischievous boy,
Tiny, but spry,
Not frightened a whit,
Leaps on a locust
And using a thread
For rein and for bit,
Clings with one hand
To a horn of its head;
And now in command,
Calls out to his band:
"Locusts, locusts,
Let us speed in our flight
Till we cover all Egypt
In a vast cloud of night."

Samekh ⟋ ס

There was a King's baker and he had a dream
Of a BASKET that held a dish.
And on the dish there was a cake,
The finest anyone could wish.

And flying round and round, a bird
Snatched the cake from off the plate,
And settling on the baker's head
Ate and ate and ate.

He may be hungry to this day
If he is not yet dead
Because the scrumptious cake he ate
Was a dream in a baker's head.

Ayin ﬡ ﬠ

*T*here came to Balaam Ben-Be'Or
The sorcerers of old Pethor,
The wise, the wily, and the old
With magic potions sevenfold,

Which made him see, EYES opening wide,
The Jews invading like a tide
The land of Moab, King Balak's land.
"Curse them all," was the King's command.

Famed for his curses, but a fool,
Proud Balaam saddled, then kicked his mule,
And cursing every curse he knew,
Swore destruction on every Jew.

But what in the end did his efforts bring?
The curses could not do a thing;
Though his evil eye flashed, blocked by the Name,
It was to him that sorrow came.

Peh ⟿ פ

Moses was only a child breast-fed
When he tossed the crown from off Pharaoh's head.

And Pharoah trembled, went weak in the knee:
This child will set his people free.

"But," said his sorcerers, looking beguiled,
"Have two bowls set before this child,

Glittering gold in the first of the bowls,
And in the second fiery coals.

If toward the first he stretch his hand,
It means his people will leave this land.

Pharaoh then can 'Off with his head,'
And the slaves will remain and all be said.

But if he choose the coals, ah then,
The child can live and our fears prove vain."

And so they brought for the child to behold
The two bowls blazing with coal and with gold.

And the king and his courtiers breathed with one wish:
Moses, Moses—the golden dish!

The choice between them was as fine as a hair.
But an angel from heaven, descending there,

Led the child's hand where the hot coals hissed,
Which the child, lifting one, fearlessly kissed.

He started to stutter when his MOUTH felt the brand,
And his people went out of Egypt land.

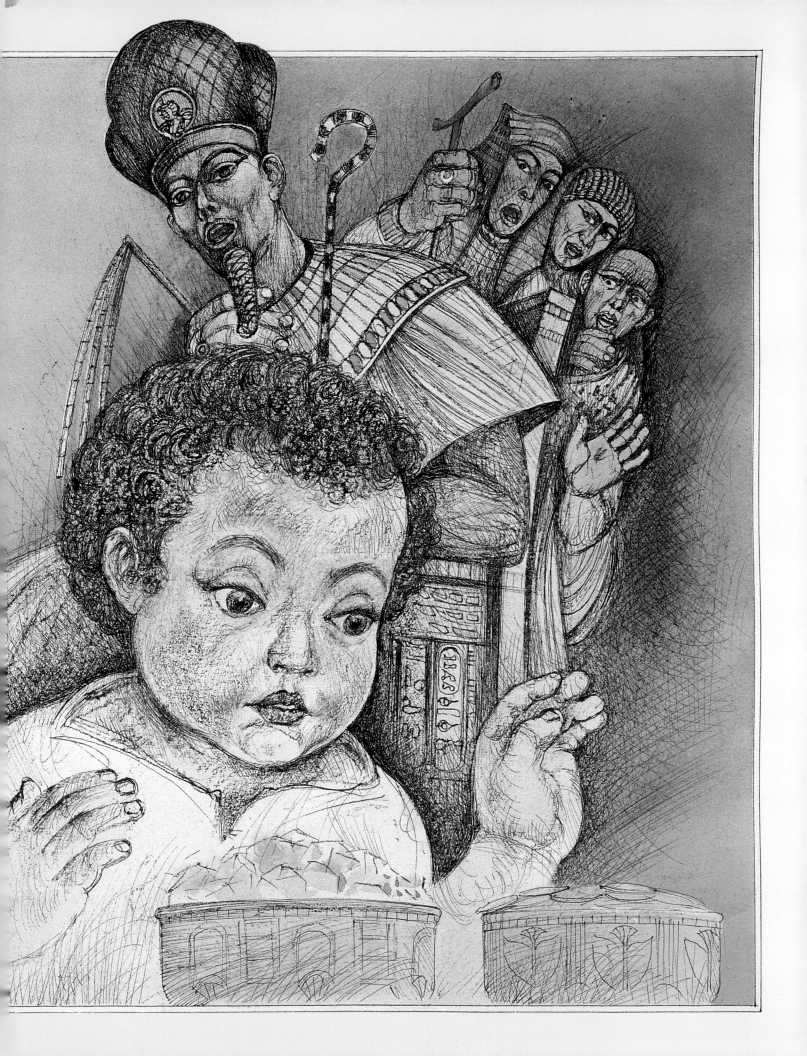

Tzadi ~ צ

I am a DEER,
And I've come down
(Light of foot)
From Jerusalem town.

The wise men said to me,
"Run, deer, run,
From city to city
And bring everyone,

Bring every child
Goodies to eat,
Raisins and almonds
And everything sweet."

But mischievous dogs
Who bit and who fought
Hunted me down
And ate all I brought.

Alas! and alas!
They ate everything
I brought for you children.
Now what shall I bring?

But I still have my horns,
So hold on to them,
And we shall go up
To Jerusalem.

Let us hurry, dear children,
And you shall be blessed
Eating almonds and raisins
And fruit of the best.

Kof ~ ק

With the Queen of Sheba,
APE came one day
To Solomon's Temple
To learn how to pray,

To grow in his knowledge
Letter by letter
And day after day.
But he liked eating better.

A beast after all,
Though he did what he could
He never learned Wisdom,
Or the knowledge of Good.

And all of his brothers
Who thought him quite other
Left him to wander
Alone in the wood.

Resh ⟨resh glyph⟩ ר

I am Goliath, the Philistine.
I have a spear. I have a bow.
Who will not fear to approach me now?

And who, O red-haired lad, are you?
And what do you think that you can do
When I hurl my spear and pierce you through?

David heard, but gave no sign
As if he hadn't been listening,
Then picked up a stone and with a sling

Smashed the HEAD of the Philistine.
Without a spear, without a bow,
Who will fear to approach him now?

Shin ⟶ ש

Perfumes, peacocks, gold-carved fish—
The ministers of old Tarshish
Brought Solomon from across the sea
A tusk of whitest IVORY.

Beautiful black boy, give to me
A tusk of whitest ivory.
Your TEETH so white put mine to scorn.
Why do you need an ivory horn?

From an elephant's tusk I shall make me
A hand, a pointer of ivory,
And I like a Rabbi shall teach God's truth—
All with the help of an elephant's tooth.

Tav ‍〰 ת

At last Uriel
Having learned well
The whole alphabet
From *Alef* to *Tav*,
Can now read the pages
Of the prophets and sages,
Just like a *Rav*.

You, too, did your best,
And now are free
To stretch out and rest
Under a tree,
While a light wind blows
From the warm south
And fat FIGS and DATES
Drop into your mouth.
The figs from the fig trees,
The dates from the palms
Are the fruit of the Prayer Book
And King David's Psalms.

Children, farewell,
And Uriel.
And I say to you
What I say to him:
May we all meet next year
In Jerusalem!

א   **ALEF**   This first letter of the alphabet naturally suggests a beginning—in this book, the first step that Uriel takes toward the world of Hebrew learning. Because *Alef* does not appear in the text of the poem, I have emphasized instead the word of which it forms a part, alphabet, *alefbet* in Hebrew.

ב   **BET**   Because the word *beit* means "house" or "temple" in Hebrew, "house" and "temple" are capitalized when they make their first appearance in the text.

ג   **GIMMEL**   No relationship in meaning exists between *Gimmel* and *gamal* (camel), but their close similarity in sound probably is the reason that Agnon made that beast the chief character of the poem.

ד   **DALET**   This letter suggests *delet*, which is Hebrew for "door," hence the stressing of that word when it makes its comic and anticlimactic appearance at the end of the poem.

ה   **HEH**   Using Abel as the central figure of this poem was probably suggested by *Heh*, which is the first letter of *Hevel*, his name in Hebrew.

ו   **VAV**   This word means "hook" in Hebrew, but in this instance, the word is only marginally connected with the meaning of the poem.

ז   **ZAYIN**   This letter suggests *zayit*, which is "olive" or "olive tree" in Hebrew, hence the references in the poem to "olive leaf," "olive tree," and "the Mount of Olives" in the poem.

ח HET   This letter must have suggested to Agnon, if arbitrarily, the Hebrew word for dream, *halom*, the first letter of which is *Het*. The dream motif is, of course, central to this poem.

ט TET   Because the curling shape of this letter suggests a serpent, the appearance of such an animal in the text is appropriate and functional.

י YOD   This letter is smuggled willy-nilly into the poem. Hardly playing a role in the text, it indicates self-indulgent humor on the part of Agnon.

כ KAF   This word literally means "pan of the scales" in Hebrew, one of several meanings.

ל LAMED   This letter suggests, somewhat far-fetchedly, the word *lapid*—in English "torch" or "flame."

מ MEM   The poem representing this letter hardly tells a story. Incantatory in style, the poem relies for its effect, both in Hebrew and in English, on the repeated use of "m" sounds in such words as "Miriam" and "Moses." The "m" sounds in *mayim* ("water") are, unfortunately, lost in translation.

נ NUN   In the original Hebrew, the poem representing this letter begins with a barrage of "n" sounds that continues through-out. The "n" effects are chiefly reproduced in the first two lines of the translation: "Noah, son of Noah,/And the son of Noah's son."

ס SAMEKH   The poem representing this letter takes for its jumping-off point the Hebrew word *sal*, meaning "basket," which begins with the same letter in Hebrew. This comic poem is a far cry from the story it derives from in the Bible, in which the baker's dream has much sadder consequences.

ע **AYIN**   This word is not only the name of a letter of the alphabet, but it is also a homonym of the word for "eye," hence the ocular theme of this poem.

פ **PEH**   This homonym for the Hebrew word for "mouth" plays a climactic role in this poem.

צ **TZADI**   This is the first letter of *zvi*, the Hebrew word for "deer."

ק **KOF**   This word is a homonym of *kof*, meaning "monkey."

ר **RESH**   This is close to the Hebrew word *rosh*, meaning "head," which in Aramaic is *resh*.

ש **SHIN**   This letter is close in sound to the Hebrew word *shen*, which means both "tooth" and "ivory."

ת **TAV**   As the last letter of the alphabet, *Tav* is a proper conclusion for Uriel's successful efforts to master the alphabet. He will now be able to continue his religious studies, the fruits of which are symbolized by the dates and figs that will fall into his mouth. The words for "dates" and "figs" in Hebrew both begin with the letter *Tav*.

תָּו

אוּרִיאֵל בֶּן תַּנְחוּם, בָּחוּר כָּאֲרָזִים,
גַּם לַמְדָן מֻפְלָג וַחֲכַם הָרָזִים,
הוּא לָמַד כָּל־הָעֵת
כָּל־הָאָלֶף בֵּית;
וּמֵאָלֶף וְעַד תָּו,
הוּא יוֹדֵעַ כְּרַב.

אַשְׁרֶיךָ שֶׁלָּמַדְתָּ תּוֹרָה עַד הֵנָּה!
וְעַתָּה לְעֵת עֶרֶב, תַּחַת הַתְּאֵנָה,
לְרוּחַ הַיּוֹם יָנוּחַ.
וְרוּחַ קָט יָפוּחַ,
וּתְאֵנָה עַל תְּאֵנָה,
דְּשֵׁנָה וּשְׁמֵנָה,
מִן הָעֵץ לְתוֹךְ פִּיו נוֹשָׁרֶת;
וְכָל־תְּאֵנָה וּתְאֵנָה לָהּ אַמָּה וָזֶרֶת.
וּבֵין לְגִימָה וּלְגִימָה,
יְזַמֵּר בִּנְעִימָה,
בְּדִקְדּוּק הַמִּלִּים,
כָּל־שִׁירֵי תְּהִלִּים.

וּמִי יִתֵּן וְנִזְכֶּה גַּם אָנוּ לְכָךְ,
לָדַעַת לְהַשְׂכִּיל וְלִלְמֹד תְּנַ"ךְ,
וְלֶאֱכֹל מִן הַתְּאֵנִים וּמִן הַתְּמָרִים
הַמְּתוּקִים שִׁבְעָתַיִם,
עִם כָּל־הַנְּעָרוֹת עִם כָּל־הַנְּעָרִים;
לַשָּׁנָה הַבָּאָה בִּירוּשָׁלַיִם.

רֵישׁ

אֲנִי גָּלְיַת רֹאשׁ פְּלֶשֶׁת,
לִי גַם כִּידוֹן, לִי גַם קֶשֶׁת,
מִי זֶה לֹא יִירָא אֵלַי לָגֶשֶׁת?

וּמִי אַתָּה נַעַר וְאַדְמוֹנִי?
כְּרֶגַע אֶתְקַע בְּךָ כִּידוֹנִי,
וּבְשָׂרְךָ אֶמְחַץ בְּשִׁרְיוֹנִי.

וּמִדֵּי דַּבְּרוֹ כָּךְ,
וְדָוִד נַעַר אַדְמוֹנִי נָרַךְ
לָקַח אֶבֶן וְיָד

אֶת־גָּלְיַת רֹאשׁ פְּלֶשֶׁת;
בְּלִי כִּידוֹן וּבְלִי קֶשֶׁת
מִי זֶה עוֹד יִירָא אֵלָיו לָגֶשֶׁת?

שִׁין

שֵׁשׁ וְשָׁנִי, דְּבַשׁ וְשֶׁמֶן,
בְּשָׂמִים רֹאשׁ וְאַבְנֵי חֵן,
שָׂרֵי תַּרְשִׁישׁ יוֹבִילוּ שַׁי,
שַׁי לִשְׁלֹמֹה אֶשְׁכַּר שֵׁן.

בָּחוּר שָׁחוֹר, יְפֵה עֵינַיִם!
שֵׁן הַפִּיל תֵּן לִי תֵּן.
יֶלֶד יָקָר, לְבֶן שְׁנַיִם!
לָמָּה לְךָ קֶרֶן שֵׁן?

אֶעֱשֶׂה לִי מִשֵּׁן הַפִּיל
יָד שֶׁל שֵׁן, יָד שֶׁל שֵׁן,
וּבַתּוֹרָה, כְּרַב וּמוֹרֶה
בְּשַׁבָּת אוֹרֶה. תֵּן לִי תֵּן.

צָדִי

אֲנִי צְבִי
קַל רַגְלַיִם,
בָּאתִי הֵנָּה
מִירוּשָׁלַיִם.

חַכְמֵי יְרוּשָׁלַיִם
אָמְרוּ לִי:
מֵעִיר לָעִיר
אוּץ, רוּץ צְבִי!

וְקַח בְּרָכָה,
שְׁקֵדִים וְצִמּוּקִים,
וְתֵן לַיְלָדִים
פֵּרוֹת מְתוּקִים.

אַךְ כְּלָבִים שׁוֹבָבִי
הָלְכוּ עִמִּי קֶרִי,
צוֹד צָדוּנִי
וַיֹּאכְלוּ כָּל־פְּרִי.

אַלְלַי לִי!
כִּי אָכְלוּ מְגָדַי,
אֲכָלוּנִי, שַׂסּוּנִי,
מָה אָבִיא לִילָדִי?

וְלִי אֵין כָּל
כִּי אִם קַרְנַיִם,
אֶחֱזוּ בָּהֶן
וְנַעֲלֶה לִירוּשָׁלַיִם.

נָאוֹצָה, נָרוּצָה
יְלָדִים נֶחְמָדִים,
וּמְצָאתֶם בְּרָכָה
כָּל־פְּרִי מְגָדִים.

קוֹף

קוֹף זֶה בָּא
עִם מַלְכַּת־שְׁבָא
לְבֵית שְׁלֹמֹה
לִלְמֹד אֱמוּנָה,
חָכְמָה וּתְבוּנָה,
דְּבַר יוֹם בְּיוֹמוֹ.
אַךְ חָכְמָה לֹא לָמַד,
לֶאֱכֹל רַק חָמַד,
כִּי הָיָה בַּעַר,
עַל כֵּן יַעֲמֹד לְבָדָד,
כָּל־אָח מִמֶּנּוּ נָדַד,
כָּל־חַיְתוֹ־יָעַר.

פֶּא

וּמֹשֶׁה עוֹד יֶלֶד יוֹנֵק שָׁדַיִם,
וַיָּסַר אֶת־הַכֶּתֶר מֵעַל רֹאשׁ מֶלֶךְ מִצְרַיִם,

וַיֶּחֱרַד פַּרְעֹה חֲרָדָה גְדוֹלָה:
זֶה הַיֶּלֶד יוֹצִיא אֶת־יִשְׂרָאֵל מִגּוֹלָה!

וַיֹּאמְרוּ לְפַרְעֹה חַרְטֻמֵּי מִצְרַיִם:
יָבִיאוּ לְפָנָיו קְעָרוֹת שְׁתַּיִם;

קְעָרָה אַחַת גֶּחָלִים בּוֹעֲרוֹת,
זָהָב פָּז בְּאַחַת הַקְּעָרוֹת,

וְהָיָה אִם יוֹשִׁיט לַזָּהָב יָדוֹ,
גּוֹאֵל לְעַמּוֹ אֱלֹהָיו יְעָדוֹ,

וְצַוֵּה פַּרְעֹה, וְאֶת רֹאשׁוֹ יָסִירוּ
מִמֶּנּוּ, עַד בֹּקֶר לֹא יוֹתִירוּ;

וְאִם לַגֶּחָלִים יוֹשֶׁט יָדוֹ – וְחָיָה,
פַּחַד פָּחַדְנוּ, וּפַחַד לֹא הָיָה.

וַיָּבִיאוּ לִפְנֵי מֹשֶׁה קְעָרוֹת שְׁתַּיִם,
גַּחֲלֵי אֵשׁ וּזְהַב פַּרְוַיִם.

וְכָל שָׂרֵי פַרְעֹה יַבִּיטוּ יוֹחִילוּ –
אֶל קַעֲרַת הַזָּהָב יְדֵי מֹשֶׁה יָגִילוּ.

וְעוֹד בֵּינוֹ וּבֵין הַזָּהָב כְּחוּט הַשַּׂעֲרָה
וּמַלְאָךְ דָּחַף יָדוֹ אֶל מוּל הַקְּעָרָה

אֲשֶׁר שָׁם גַּחֶלֶת תְּפַזֵּז וְתִיו,
וַיִּקָּחֶהָ מֹשֶׁה וַיַּגַּע אֶל פִּיו.

וַיְהִי מֹשֶׁה כְּבַד פֶּה וַעֲרַל שְׂפָתַיִם –
וַיּוֹצֵא אֶת עַמּוֹ יִשְׂרָאֵל מֵאֶרֶץ מִצְרַיִם.

עַיִן

אֶל בִּלְעָם בֶּן־בְּעוֹר,
הַקּוֹסֵם בְּעִיר פְּתוֹר,
בָּאוּ זְקֵנִים וַחֲכָמִים
עִם תִּשְׁעָה קַבִּין קְסָמִים.

הוֹי חוֹזֶה גְּלוּי עֵינַיִם!
עַם יָצָא מִמִּצְרַיִם,
וַיְכַס אֶת־עֵין הָאָרֶץ,
קְרָץ עֲלֵימוֹ קָרֶץ!

וַיַּחֲבֹשׁ אֶת־אֲתוֹנוֹ
וַיַּעַף בַּהֲדַר גְּאוֹנוֹ,
וּפִיו מָלֵא אָלָה
לַעֲשׂוֹת בְּיִשְׂרָאֵל כָּלָה.

אַךְ קִלְלָתוֹ כְּאַיִן,
וְאֵל שָׁתַם לוֹ עַיִן;
עֵינוֹ הָיְתָה רָעָה
צָרָה עָלָיו בָּאָה.

סָמֶךְ

חֲלוֹם חָלַם שַׂר הָאוֹפִים:
סַלִּים רָאָה בַּחֲלוֹמוֹ,
וּבַסַּלִּים מַעֲשֵׂה אוֹפֶה,
עוּגוֹת סֹלֶת, רָקִיק בֶּן יוֹמוֹ.

וְהָעוֹף סוֹבֵב, סוֹבֵב
אֶת־הַסַּלִּים בַּמְּחוּגָה
וּמֵעַל רֹאשׁ שַׂר הָאוֹפִים,
אָכֹל יֹאכַל עוּגָה עוּגָה.

וְאִם לֹא מֵת עוֹד הָעוֹף,
יִרְעַב עַד הַיּוֹם;
כִּי הָעוּגוֹת אֲשֶׁר אָכַל,
הָיוּ רַק חֲלוֹם.

מֵם

לִיאוֹר מִצְרַיִם,
לִשְׁאֹב מַיִם,
יָרֹד יָרְדָה מִרְיָם
וּמַיִם הֵבִיאָה,
מִרְיָם הַנְּבִיאָה,
לִרְחֹץ אֶת־אָחִיהָ,
אֶת־אָחִיהָ
אֶת־מֹשֶׁה.

הַיּוֹם רַד,
וּבַכַּד
מַיִם, מַיִם, מַיִם;
מַיִם הֵבִיאָה
מִרְיָם הַנְּבִיאָה
לִרְחֹץ אֶת־אָחִיהָ,
אֶת־אָחִיהָ
אֶת־מֹשֶׁה.

נוּן

נֹחַ בֶּן נֹחַ, בֶּן־בֶּן נֹחַ,
בְּגַן וּבְנִיר אֵין לוֹ מָנוֹחַ.
הִנֵּה הָאַרְבֶּה,
הַרְבֵּה, הַרְבֵּה;
נַתְרָנִים, נַקְרָנִים,
נַבְחָנִים, נַשְׁכָנִים,
כָּל־נִטְעֵי נַעֲמָנִים
יְכֻסּוּ כַּעֲנָנִים.
נַעַר קָטָן,
בְּכוֹר שָׂטָן,
בֶּן רֶגַע הוּא קוֹשֵׁר לְאַרְבֶּה נִימָה,
וְהִנֵּה הוּא נֶאֱחָז בֵּין הַקַּרְנַיִם.
אַרְבֶּה בֶּן אַרְבֶּה, פְּעָמֶיךָ הָרִימָה!
נַעֲלֶה וְנִסַּע בְּכָל־אֶרֶץ מִצְרַיִם.

לָמֶד

אֶת־צַמְרִי וּפִשְׁתִּי
שְׁלַל הַפְּלִשְׁתִּי,
וְשׁוּעָל בִּגְבוּלִי,
זָלַל דָּלַל יְבוּלִי.

הַס! שִׁמְשׁוֹן נָתַן קוֹל, וּמִיָּמִין וּמִשְּׂמֹאל
שְׁלֹשׁ מֵאוֹת שׁוּעָלִים, בְּהוֹלִים וּמְבֹהָלִים,
יָבוֹאוּ לְפָנָיו וַיְכַשְׁכְּשׁוּ בְּזָנָב.

מַה יָּפוּ פַּעֲמֵיכֶם,
שׁוּעָלִים נִפְתָּלִים!
לַפִּידִים בְּזַנְבוֹתֵיכֶם,
אוֹרוֹת וּדְגָלִים.

וַיֶּפֶן זָנָב אֶל זָנָב,
וַיָּשֶׂם בַּתָּוֶךְ לַפִּיד גָּפְרִית וּפִשְׁתִּים,
וַיַּבְעֶר אֵשׁ בַּלַּפִּידִים, וַיְשַׁלְּחֵם מִלְּפָנָיו
בְּקָמוֹת פְּלִשְׁתִּים.

הֵימִינוּ, הַשְׂמְאִילוּ,
בְּגָדִישׁ וּבְקָמָה.
צַהֲלוּ וְגִילוּ
כָּל־עוֹד בָּכֶם נְשָׁמָה.

בְּכַרְמֵי פְלֶשֶׁת, גַּם שָׁם בַּשִּׁבֳּלִים
הֵילִילוּ וָחוּלוּ, רָקְדוּ כְּעַתּוּדִים,
לְאוֹר הַלַּפִּידִים יָנוּסוּ הַצְּלָלִים,
שִׂמְחָה וְשָׂשׂוֹן, אוֹר לַיְּהוּדִים.

כ

כַּף מֹאזְנַיִם,
כַּף מֹאזְנַיִם,
כַּשְׂדִּים נִלְחָמִים
עַל יְרוּשָׁלַיִם.

כַּף מֹאזְנַיִם,
כַּף מֹאזְנַיִם,
וְיִרְמְיָה אָסוּר
בִּנְחֻשְׁתַּיִם.

כַּף מֹאזְנַיִם,
כַּף מֹאזְנַיִם,
וּדְבַר יְיָ
פַּעַם וּשְׁתַּיִם.

כַּף מֹאזְנַיִם,
כַּף מֹאזְנַיִם,
קְנֵה לְךָ שָׂדֶה
בִּסְבִיבֵי יְרוּשָׁלַיִם.

כַּף מֹאזְנַיִם,
כַּפּוֹת שְׁתַּיִם,
שָׂדוֹת יִקָּנוּ
בִּירוּשָׁלַיִם.

שֶׁקֶל קֹדֶשׁ
בְּכַף מֹאזְנַיִם —
רַחֵם יְיָ
צִיּוֹן וִירוּשָׁלַיִם.

טית

וְאֶת־יוֹסֵף הִשְׁלִיכוּ
לְבוֹר שֶׁל נְחָשִׁים,
וּלְכָל־נָחָשׁ וְנָחָשׁ
שִׁבְעָה שִׁבְעָה רָאשִׁים.

וּנְחָשִׁים מִתְפַּתְּלִים
כְּזַיִן, כְּחֵית,
שָׁם נָחָשׁ עַל אָזְנוֹ
מִתְפַּתֵּל כְּטֵית.

הִתְפַּתֵּל הַנָּחָשׁ,
וְרָחַשׁ וְלָחַשׁ;
בִּשְׂפָתַי אֵין כַּחַשׁ
לַחַשׁ הַנָּחָשׁ:

בְּטַח בַּיְיָ וַעֲשֵׂה טוֹב
גַּם כִּי אוֹיְבֶיךָ רַבִּים,
וְאַל תִּירָא וְאַל תֵּחַת
מִנְּחָשִׁים, מֵעַקְרַבִּים.

יוֹד

וְהָיָה
בְּאַחֲרִית הַיָּמִים,
זְאֵב וְשֶׂה תָּמִים
אֶל רַב אֶחָד
יֵלְכוּ הַחַדְרָה;
וּבַחֲמֵשׁ אֶחָד
יִלְמְדוּ הַסִּדְרָה.
וְנָמֵר עִם גְּדִי,
וּכְפִיר וּמְרִיא,
שָׂפָה אַחַת
וּדְבָרִים אֲחָדִים
לוֹמְדִים כְּאֶחָד
בְּגַן יְלָדִים.
וְגָמוּל יַפְרִיחַ
נָחָשׁ בָּרִיחַ,
וְעַל חֵר פֶּתֶן
יָדוֹ הָדָה.
נִשְׁלְמָה אוֹת יוֹד
וְתַמָּה הָאַגָּדָה.

חֵית

עוֹד לֹא עָבַר הַלַּיְל, עוֹד הַבֹּקֶר לֹא בָּא,
וּמִשְׁנָתוֹ חָרַד יוֹסֵף, חֲלוֹם חָלַם וָזָע.
דְּמָמָה וָשֶׁקֶט, אֵין קֶשֶׁב וְאֵין קוֹל;
דּוּמָם יִתְלַחֵשׁ עַל חוֹף יַמִּים הַחוֹל.
וּבַמֶּרְחַקֵּי אֵין סוֹף, בֵּין מִפְלְשֵׂי עָבִים,
אוֹר הַלְּבָנָה זוֹרֵחַ.
וְהִנֵּה מִשְׁתַּחֲוִים לוֹ אַחַד־עָשָׂר כּוֹכָבִים,
גַּם שֶׁמֶשׁ וְיָרֵחַ.

יַבִּיט אֶל יָמִין וְיַבִּיט אֶל שְׂמֹאל—
דְּמָמָה וָשֶׁקֶט, אֵין קֶשֶׁב וְאֵין קוֹל;
אֶחָיו יָנוּחוּ אַחֲרֵי עֲמַל הַיּוֹם
וּלְבַדּוֹ הוּא עֵר, וְחָרֵד מֵחֲלוֹם.
וּבַמֶּרְחַקֵּי אֵין סוֹף אוֹר הַלְּבָנָה זוֹרֵחַ
בֵּין מִפְלְשֵׂי עָבִים.
וְהִנֵּה מִשְׁתַּחֲוִים לוֹ שֶׁמֶשׁ וְיָרֵחַ
וְאַחַד־עָשָׂר כּוֹכָבִים.

יַבִּיט אֶל כּוֹכָב וְיַבִּיט אֶל אָח—
פְּנֵי אָח כִּפְנֵי כּוֹכָב, פְּנֵי כּוֹכָב כִּפְנֵי אָח.
הִנֵּה יָצָא הַיָּרֵחַ מִבֵּין מִפְלְשֵׂי עָב,
פְּנֵי אִמּוֹ—פְּנֵי יָרֵחַ, פְּנֵי שֶׁמֶשׁ—פְּנֵי אָב.
וְאִמּוֹ כְּבָר מֵתָה, אֵיךְ בָּאָה הֲלוֹם?
וּבַלַּיְלָה שֶׁמֶשׁ לֹא יָאִיר!
וְאַחַי יִשְׂנָאוּנִי. מַה זֶּה הַחֲלוֹם,
הֲיִשְׁתַּחֲוֶה רַב לְצָעִיר?

וָו

עֲצֵי שִׁטִּים עֶשְׂרִים קְרָשִׁים;
עוֹרוֹת אֵילִים, עוֹרוֹת תְּחָשִׁים;
קָו, קָו, קָו,
וָו, וָו, וָו,
וָוֵי הָעַמּוּדִים,
מַעֲשֵׂה חָרָשׁ
זָהָב וּנְחֹשֶׁת
וָוֵי הָעַמּוּדִים.

קַרְסֵי זָהָב וְלוּלָאוֹת
יְרִיעוֹת עִזִּים וְטַבָּעוֹת,
צָו, צָו, צָו,
וָו, וָו, וָו,
וָוֵי הָעַמּוּדִים.
וּבְצַלְאֵל יוֹשֵׁב
רוֹקֵעַ וְחוֹשֵׁב,
וָוֵי הָעַמּוּדִים.

זַיִן

זֹאת הַיּוֹנָה מַה בְּפִיהָ?
עֲלֵה זַיִת בְּפִיהָ!
לְתֵבַת נֹחַ מִכְתָּב זֶה
יוֹנָה זוֹ הֵבִיאָה.

שָׁלֹחַ שָׁלְחוּ לוֹ הָעֵצִים
מִירוּשָׁלַיִם מֵהַר הַזַּיִת:
רַב לְךָ נְדוֹד בְּכָל־הָעוֹלָם
בְּנֵה־לְךָ בְּצִיּוֹן בַּיִת!

דָּלֶת

וְיוֹסֵף הוּא הַשַּׁלִּיט
בְּכָל־אֶרֶץ מִצְרַיִם;
וַיָּבוֹא כָּל־הָעָם,
וַיִּשְׁתַּחֲווּ לוֹ אַפַּיִם.

וַיָּבִיאוּ אֶל יוֹסֵף
כֶּסֶף וְזָהָב,
וַיִּתֵּן לָהֶם בַּר
לִשְׁבֹּר הָרָעָב.

וְגַם אֲחֵי יוֹסֵף
אֶל יוֹסֵף בָּאוּ
שָׁוְא תְּבַקְשֵׁם
הֵמָּה לֹא יֵרָאוּ.

כִּי הֵמָּה עִם יוֹסֵף
בְּבֵיתוֹ שָׁם, יָלֶד!
וְאַתָּה תִּרְאֶה
רַק אֶת־הַדֶּלֶת.

הֵא

וַיְהִי הֶבֶל רוֹעֶה
בַּיָּמִים הָהֵם,
וַיַּרְא צֹאן תּוֹעֶה,
וַיְהִי לָהּ לְאֵם;

וַיִּקָּחֶהָ וַיִּרְעֶהָ,
וַיִּתֶּן לָהּ מַיִם
וַיַּאֲכִילֶהָ, וַיַּשְׁקֶהָ,
וַיָּנַח בַּצָּהֳרָיִם.

גִּימֶל

נֹחַ אִישׁ צַדִּיק תָּמִים
עָשָׂה תֵּבַת גֹּפֶר,
מִבַּיִת וּמִחוּץ
כָּפַר אוֹתָהּ בַּכֹּפֶר.

גָּמָל, גָּמָל מַהֵר, מַהֵר
בַּקֵּשׁ לְךָ מָנוֹחַ
הִנֵּה שָׁם בַּצֹּהַר
דּוֹאֵג לְךָ הַזָּקֵן נֹחַ!

וַיָּבוֹאוּ מִכָּל־הַחַי
זָכָר וּנְקֵבָה
מִן הָעוֹף וּמִן הַבְּהֵמָה
בָּאוּ אֶל הַתֵּבָה.

וְהַגָּמָל גְּבַהּ רַגְלַיִם
מִתְגָּרֵד קְצָת בִּגְרוֹנוֹ,
מַעֲלֶה גֵּרָה וְגוֹנֵחַ
וּמְגַמְגֵּם לוֹ בִּלְשׁוֹנוֹ:

וַיָּבוֹאוּ מִכָּל־הַחַי,
הַכֹּל בָּא בְּעִתּוֹ,
רַק הַגָּמָל גְּדוֹל הַגּוּף
הוֹלֵךְ לוֹ לְאִטּוֹ.

הֵן יֵשׁ בָּאָרֶץ
חַיָּה רְפַת רַגְלַיִם;
חָגָב, חַרְגּוֹל, גּוֹזָל
רְצוּץ כְּנָפַיִם,

אֶעֱמֹד רֶגַע וּבְלִי פֶגַע
יִרְכְּבוּ עַל גַּבִּי
עָלַי וְעַל דַּבַּשְׁתִּי
אֶל תֵּבַת נֹחַ רַבִּי.

אָלֶף

לְאוֹר הַנֵּר, מֵעֵת לְעֵת
אוּרִיאֵל הַקָּטָן יוֹשֵׁב,
וּלְפָנָיו סֵפֶר אָלֶף־בֵּית,
וְהוּא הוֹגֶה בּוֹ וְחוֹשֵׁב:

אוֹתִיּוֹת עֶשְׂרִים וּשְׁתַּיִם
הוֹי מָה רַב! מָה רַב!
וּמִלְּאָךְ מִן הַשָּׁמַיִם
לוֹחֵשׁ מִן הַדַּף:

הַיּוֹם אוֹת, וּמָחָר אוֹת!
בְּלִי פַחַד וּבְלִי מוֹרָא -
וְאִם עוֹשֶׂה אַתָּה זֹאת
תֵּדַע כָּל־הַתּוֹרָה!

בֵּית

בֵּית הַמִּקְדָּשׁ שְׁלֹמֹה בָּנָה,
בְּעִיר הַקֹּדֶשׁ בִּירוּשָׁלַיִם;
בִּשְׁמוֹנִים שָׁנָה וְאַרְבַּע מֵאוֹת שָׁנָה,
לְצֵאת יִשְׂרָאֵל מִמִּצְרָיִם.

וַיִּבְנֵהוּ שֶׁבַע שָׁנִים,
לְאֵל יִשְׂרָאֵל בְּרָכָה;
שְׁמוֹנִים אֶלֶף חָצְבוּ אֲבָנִים
וְנוֹשֵׂא סַבָּל בַּמְּלָאכָה-

בְּלִי מִסְפָּר וּבְלִי מִנְיָן
שִׁבְעִים אֶלֶף אִישׁ,
וְהַנִּצָּבִים עַל הַבִּנְיָן
קוֹרְאִים: חִישׁ, חִישׁ, חִישׁ!

בַּיִת נִבְנֶה לַשְּׁכִינָה
בְּרֹאשׁ כָּל־הֶהָרִים
וּלְשׁוֹנָם מָלֵא רִנָּה
וְעוֹבְדִים וְשָׁרִים.

שְׁמוּאֵל יוֹסֵף עַגְנוֹן

סֵפֶר הָאוֹתִיּוֹת